Let's Make - Believe

Written by P. Taylor Copeland
Illustrated by Suzi Bliss Kyle

Let's Make-Believe
2002 Grammy Time™ Books/P. Taylor Copeland
P.O. Box 639 San Luis Obispo, CA 93406-0639
Message/Fax (805) 541-3515
www.grammytimebooks.com

Designed by
(KRAFTWERK) DESIGN

Special thanks to our friend Tracy Taylor

Printed in China

ISBN 0-9712675-1-0

For Oliver

I am your Grammy,
Your playmate and friend;
My **love** has no boundary,
My love has no end.

With your hand in mine
We link **future** to **past**;
Generations joined—
Our time unsurpassed.

I **treasure** each minute,
Though sometimes **too few**;
The world of a child
Offers uncluttered view.

Discovery and wonder,
Imagination and play,
Your giggles and laughs
Bring **joy** to my day.

Whether **snuggle-time** stories
Or visiting the **zoo**,
We catch our own memories—
Memories for two.

xoxo and lots of love

A playdate with Grammy

Is all about FUN _

Let's make-believe

LET'S COME ALL UNDONE.

We can act like an ape

Or a chimp in a tree;

Let's be a monkey —

What else can we be?

Bear cubs are playful
And prance all about,
Let's join the party,
Let's sing and let's shout.

We gallop and run,

Go fast like a horse,

But **wait** we have stripes—

We're zebras of course.

GRRRR says the lion

Wandering proud-

Let's growl together;
Let's roar really loud.

Look, there's a tiger
On top of the bed;
Let's crawl along,
We'll creep up ahead.

Here comes the alligator

Awake from a nap—

Let's follow behind,

Snippety-SNAP!

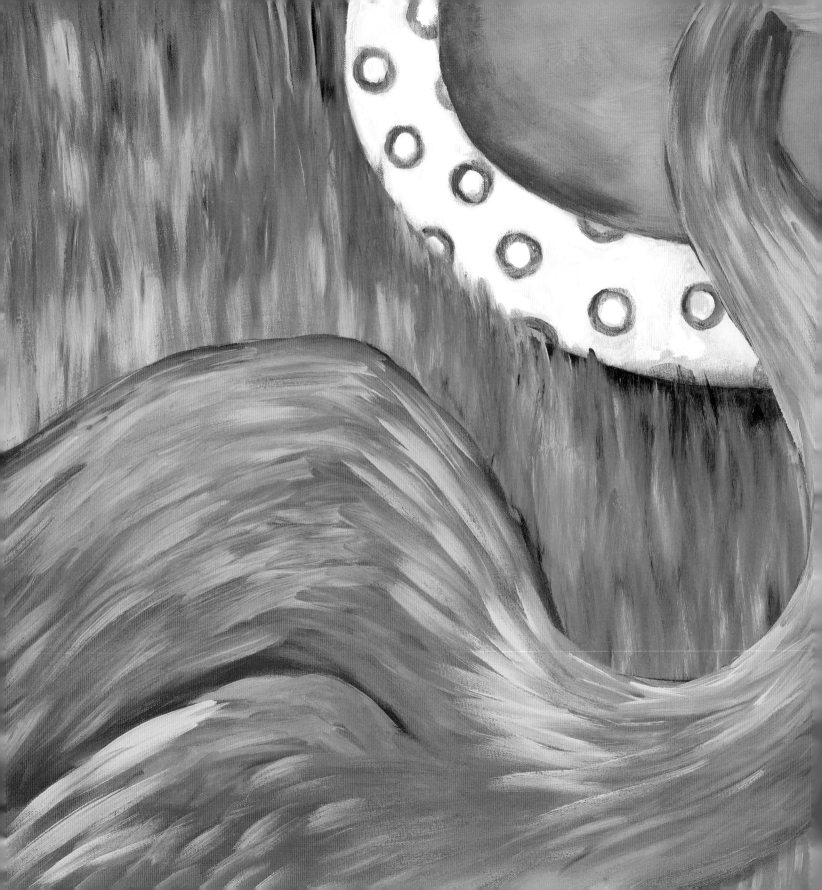

We paint a bright picture

Red, yellow and blue;

An orange flamingo?

A green kangaroo?

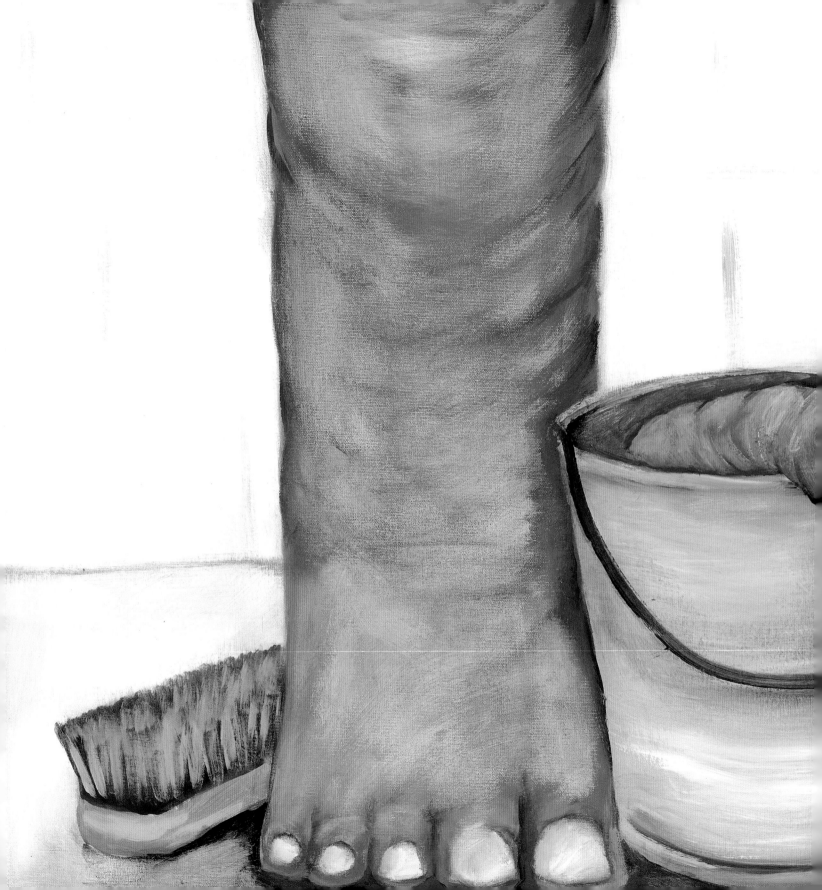

We splash in the water,
Get sprayed by the hose.
But wait just a minute—
That's an elephant's nose.

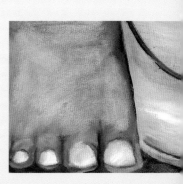

Hippos swim shyly

Sneaking a peek~

Let's play their game,

Let's play hide~"n~seek.

The long-necked giraffe
Sees both far and near,
"It's a wonderful view
With my head way up here."

We spread out our arms;
We take a quick flight—

We're a **bird**, we're a plane,
We soar with delight.

"What about me?"

The rhino says with a sigh,

We'll visit again-

But for now it's good-bye.

More From Grammy Time Books...

Just You And Me

I Liked You At Ten...I'll Like You Again

(visit grammytimebooks.com for more information)

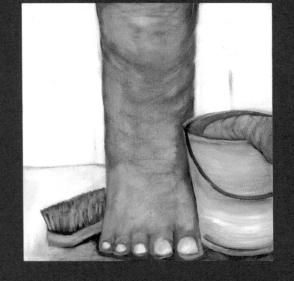

Let's Make